THE RICERCARS
OF THE
BOURDENEY CODEX

RECENT RESEARCHES IN THE MUSIC OF THE RENAISSANCE

James Haar, general editor

A-R Editions, Inc., publishes seven series of musicological editions
that present music brought to light in the course of current research:

Recent Researches in the Music of the Middle Ages and Early Renaissance
Charles M. Atkinson, general editor

Recent Researches in the Music of the Renaissance
James Haar, general editor

Recent Researches in the Music of the Baroque Era
Christoph Wolff, general editor

Recent Researches in the Music of the Classical Era
Eugene K. Wolf, general editor

Recent Researches in the Music of the Nineteenth and Early Twentieth Centuries
Rufus Hallmark and D. Kern Holoman, general editors

Recent Researches in American Music
H. Wiley Hitchcock, general editor

Recent Researches in the Oral Traditions of Music
Philip V. Bohlman, general editor

Each *Recent Researches* edition is devoted to works
by a single composer or to a single genre of composition.
The contents are chosen for their potential interest to scholars
and performers, then prepared for publication according to the
standards that govern the making of all reliable historical editions.

Subscribers to any of these series, as well as patrons of subscribing institutions,
are invited to apply for information about the "Copyright-Sharing Policy"
of A-R Editions, Inc., under which policy any part of an edition
may be reproduced free of charge for study or performance.

For information contact

A-R EDITIONS, INC.
801 Deming Way
Madison, Wisconsin 53717

(608) 836-9000

RECENT RESEARCHES IN THE MUSIC OF THE RENAISSANCE • VOLUME 89

THE RICERCARS OF THE BOURDENEY CODEX

Giaches Brumel [?],
Fabrizio Dentice, Anonymous

Edited by Anthony Newcomb

 A-R Editions, Inc.
Madison

Performance parts and a keyboard score are available from the pub-
lisher.

© 1991 by A-R Editions, Inc.
Printed in the United States of America

Library of Congress Cataloging-in-Publication Data

The Ricercars of the Bourdeney codex / Giaches Brumel (?), Fabrizio
  Dentice, anonymous ; edited by Anthony Newcomb.
    1 score. — (Recent researches in the music of the renaissance.
  ISSN 0486-123X ; v. 89)
    For 4 unspecified instruments (except one ricercar for 5
  unspecified instruments).
      Edited from Paris, Bibliothèque nationale, Rés. Vma ms. 851.
      Includes pref. and critical notes.
      Includes bibliographical references.
      Contains 14 ricercars attributed to Giaches Brumel, Ricercar del
  settimo tono by Fabrizio Dentice, and 2 anon. ricercars.
      ISBN 0-089579-264-8
      1. Canons, fugues, etc. (Unspecified instruments (4))—Scores.
  2. Canons, fugues, etc. (Unspecified instruments (5))—Scores.
  I. Newcomb, Anthony, 1943–   II. Brumel, Giaches, d. 1564.
  III. Bourdeney codex.   IV. Series.
  M2.R2384   vol. 89
  [M990]   91-754892
                                                    CIP
                                                    M

Contents

Preface

If the dating and attribution proposed for the ricercars in this volume are correct, these pieces constitute one of our largest and most significant sources for the early imitative ricercar. Moreover, they mark the beginning of a new style—literally a new school—of ricercar composition that was to culminate in the imitative works of Girolamo Frescobaldi about one-half century later and to be passed on through his works to the northern and southern German keyboard composers of the next century and beyond. Finally, the works are intrinsically of high value, showing an inventive musical intellect enjoying the challenge of making a musical coherence and shape that is independent of text or social function.[1]

The Source

These ricercars are preserved in Paris, Bibliothèque nationale, Rés. Vma ms. 851, a late sixteenth-century manuscript containing 469 pieces of polyphony. The codex was first summarily described by Nanie Bridgman and François Lesure soon after its acquisition by the Bibliothèque nationale from the heirs of Clarisse Bourdeney in 1954.[2] Oscar Mischiati published a more exhaustive analysis and an inventory of its contents in 1975.[3] (It is this inventory to which the M-numbers throughout this edition refer.) The Bourdeney Codex, written in score,[4] is a compilation of often fully texted madrigals, motets, and masses by composers from Josquin and Mouton through Pallavicino and Marenzio. Mischiati concludes convincingly from an analysis of the repertoire in the codex that it comes from the Po valley, probably the lower Po valley. Connections with Ravenna seem particularly strong.[5] Some jottings at the end of the codex (which have nothing directly to do with its preparation and hence cannot date it precisely) bear the date 1600, which can thus be taken as a *terminus ante quem*. Bridgman and Lesure find the watermark of the paper to be identical with that of paper used in documents of 1575–76 in Fabriano.[6] The codex contains among its later pieces madrigals from Marenzio's second book *a 6* (1584) and Pallavicino's third book *a 5* (1585). Since neither of these composers seems to have let pieces drift around unpublished for long, we should probably place the copying of at least the latter part of the codex after 1585, the date of Pallavicino's third book.

The Bourdeney Codex contains among its 469 compositions a small amount of instrumental music, part of which appears as a series of sixteen untexted four-voice pieces and one untexted five-voice piece—interrupted by a five-voice motet by Animuccia—beginning with M295 and listed in table 1 below.

The Chigi Concordances

In his inventory of the codex, Mischiati noted that four of the present ricercars were identical with four pieces called *"fantasie"* in a pair of manuscript fascicles now in the Chigi collection of the Biblioteca Apostolica Vaticana. In these fascicles the pieces are attributed to "Giaches."[7] In an article of 1960 Edward Lowinsky had called attention to the four *fantasie* in the Chigi fascicles and proposed the identification of "Giaches" with Giaches Brumel, who was court organist at Ferrara from 1532 until his death in 1564.[8] Soon afterward, Carol MacClintock pointed out that the ricercar on *la sol fa re mi* in the Chigi fascicles was not, as Lowinsky had claimed, the same piece as a ricercar on *la sol fa re mi* attributed to "Giaches organista" in a manuscript lute tablature now in Uppsala.[9] She proposed instead an attribution to Giaches de Wert, *maestro di cappella* at the ducal chapel in Mantua from 1565 until his death in 1596.[10] The attribution of the Chigi pieces to Wert has not been challenged since MacClintock's article; it was accepted both by Mischiati in his inventory of the Bourdeney Codex and by the present author in a stylistic and critical study of one of the present pieces (no. 5), as copied from the Chigi fascicle.[11]

Dating and Attribution

I had occasion to study all seventeen of the anonymous ricercars in the Bourdeney Codex (including, of course, the four pieces identical with the four in the Chigi fascicles) as part of a survey of the ensemble and keyboard ricercar/fantasia in the sixteenth century. This study led to two conclusions. First, most of the Bourdeney ricercars (referred to below as the "principal group") were composed around 1560 by a single composer, the same who had written the four pieces also found in the Chigi fascicles, and this composer was in all probability Giaches Brumel. Second, a group of three stylistically distinct ricercars (referred to below as the "Appendix pieces")—one attributed in the manuscript to Fabrizio Dentice, the other two anonymous—is embedded in the midst of these stylistically homogeneous ricercars by Brumel.[12]

TABLE 1

Inventory and Mode of the Bourdeney Ricercars

Edition Number	Mischiati Number	System	*Ambitus**	Final (lowest voice)	Mode
Principal Group					
1	295	♭	c_1	d	9
2	296	♮	c_1	e	[3]
3	297	♮	c_1	E	[3]
4	298	♮	g_2	a	[(1 or) 9]
5	299	♮	g_2	f	[5]
6	300	♮	g_2	c	[(6 or) 12]
7	305	♮	c_1	d	1
8	306	♮	c_1	d	1
9	307	♭	c_1	G	2
10	308	♭	c_1	G	2
11	309	♮**	c_1	e	3
12	310	♭	c_1	A	4
13	311	♭	c_1	F	12
14	312	♭	g_2	g	[1]
Appendix Pieces					
15	301	♮	c_1	D	[1]
16	302	♮	g_2	g	[7]
17	303	♭	c_1	[G]	[2]

*c_1 = c_3 c_4 f_4 (top to bottom)
g_2 = g_2 c_2 c_3 (or c_4) f_3 (top to bottom)
no. 14: g_2 c_2 c_3 c_3 f_3 (top to bottom)
**Staves 1 and 3 have anomalous flats in the first system

If the first of these conclusions is correct—that is, if the Bourdeney pieces were written in Ferrara during the later 1550s or early 1560s—then the codex takes its place as one of our most important sources for the mid-century ricercar. In particular, these pieces bring striking stylistic innovations to the generic idea of the ricercar. In them the ricercar moves far from the motet, most particularly in the strict limitation of its thematic material and in the severely intellectual manipulations and variations to which this limited amount of material is subjected.

These pieces also mark the beginning of a new and important school of abstract instrumental composition. We can now understand that it was in this school—which continues in the ricercars of Luzzasco Luzzaschi (Brumel's successor as court organist at Ferrara) and those of Luzzaschi's admirer Giovanni de' Macque (who worked in Rome and Naples)—that the contrapuntal style of Luzzaschi's pupil Girolamo Frescobaldi was formed.

Principal Group

Characteristic features of the unified principal group of fourteen ricercars tend to support a mid-century origin. The length of these pieces is a throwback to the dimensions found in ricercars of the 1540s. Specifically, each of these fourteen pieces totals over one hundred tactus units (the breve for all but no. 14, which, like its model, is notated in C instead of ₵ and hence has a semibreve tactus). Nine of the fourteen pieces are between 180 and 250 breves long, which is even longer than Annibale Padovano's ricercars of 1556 and harks back to the ricercars by Jacques Buus published in 1547 and 1549.[13] This in itself makes a date later than 1565 unlikely: the length of a sixteenth-century ricercar (unlike, for example, that of a motet) is a rather reliable index of its date, for the imitative ricercar as a genre quickly became highly self-conscious and convention-bound. Among these conventions was length, which became consistently shorter between 1550 and 1575, settling at about one hundred breves by the late 1570s.[14] Ricercars as long as the Bourdeney pieces were virtually unheard of in the last quarter of the century. For example, the printer Giacomo Vincenti, reprinting in 1591 two ricercars from Padovano's collection of 1556, was moved to cut them drastically—to fifty-three and ninety breves from originals of two to three times this length.[15]

A mid-century origin is also suggested by the numerous similarities, both stylistic and external, between the main group of Bourdeney pieces and Padovano's book of ricercars of 1556, which apparently was widely influential.[16] Among the external similarities are the following:

the modal labeling of some of the pieces (Padovano's was the first published collection of ricercars to be so labeled; such labeling became increasingly conventional in the ricercar collections of the second half of the century; see table 2);

the presence in both collections of pieces or sections of pieces based on *la sol fa re mi*;

the presence in both collections of pieces based on the successive phrases of a well-known chant.[17]

In its musical style Padovano's collection brings together for the first time most elements of the mature imitative ricercar/fantasia: a dignified and homogeneous level of rhythmic activity; diatonic, largely conjunct thematic material; the linking of thematic material by means of subtle motivic interconnection and variation; and the variation of thematic material by constant rhythmic permutation and by learned devices (augmentation, diminution, inversion, and stretto). It is this generic style that forms the basis of the style of the Bourdeney pieces.

For all its points in common with the Padovano collection, however, the style of the principal group of Bourdeney ricercars differs markedly from Padovano's style in various ways. The Bourdeney ricercars use Padovano's learned devices and thematic linking by motivic variation, but they do so much more insistently. And they add to Padovano's learned devices the frequent use of *inganno* (the first use that I know of this device in the four-voice ricercar).[18] To a much greater extent than Padovano's pieces, they work with two or more bits of thematic material at once, often stating a compound set of thematic materials at the beginning and working with this set throughout the rest of the piece, developing it by various techniques of motivic variation. Finally, the Bourdeney ricercars have extraordinary thematic density (see table 3). With two or three bits of thematic material in play at once, and with the possibility of wide-ranging rhythmic variation of this material, these ricercars move toward a state in which most melodic material at any given time is thematically derived—a state that will come closer and closer to realization in the ricercars of Luzzaschi and Macque and in the fantasies of Frescobaldi. The style inaugurated by the Bourdeney ricercars is thus quite distinct from the Venetian style of ricercar practiced by Padovano and continuing after Padovano, a style seen in the largely posthumous prints of Claudio Merulo, Andrea Gabrieli, and Sperindio Bertoldo.[19]

The hypothesis proposed here, then, is that a distinct style of imitative ricercar split off from the original Venetian style of the 1540s and early 1550s—the style of Willaert, Buus, and Padovano. The earliest pieces in this new and distinct style are the Bourdeney ricercars, which seem on stylistic evidence to come from the later 1550s or early 1560s.

In determining who is the "Giaches" to whom some of these pieces are attributed in the Chigi fascicles, one does not need to rely on stylistic evidence alone. If one accepts a mid-century date for the Bourdeney pieces, as is indicated both by their length and by the similarities to the Padovano collection, this would agree on the grounds of simple chronology much more easily with the authorship of Giaches Brumel than with that of Giaches Wert. Brumel, who may have been the same person as the "Jacques Brunel" who left a post as organist at the cathedral of Rouen in December 1524, became organist at the court of Ferrara at some time before August 1532. From 1547 to 1558 he would have worked there under Cipriano da Rore, one of whose madrigals is parodied in the last ricercar of the group (no. 14). Brumel retired from active service at the court some time between 1559 and March 1564, during which period Luzzaschi had taken up a position as second organist at the court. Brumel died in May 1564.

A number of factors other than the purely chronological tend to support the hypothesis that Giaches Brumel wrote the principal group of Bourdeney ricercars.

First, Brumel was widely famous as an organist and composer of keyboard music by mid-century.[20] No evidence indicates that Wert was ever known as either. In fact, apart from MacClintock's attribution to Wert of the four Chigi ricercars, no instrumental music of any kind has been credited to the later composer. All known compositions by Brumel, on the other hand (and exclusive of the Bourdeney pieces), are instrumental ricercars or organ masses.

Second, Brumel's presumably much earlier ricercars in the Castell'Arquato organ tablatures and in the Uppsala lute tablature (both manuscript), though stylistically and generically less advanced and self-assured than the Bourdeney pieces, contain foreshadowings of the style of the Bourdeney pieces. In the case of the Castell'Arquato ricercars, one of the two ricercars by Brumel is the most advanced imitative piece in the collection, in the sense that it comes closest to the imitative-point ricercar of the 1540s—further indication that Brumel was at the forefront of the organist-composers experimenting with the new genre at that time.[21]

Third, Claudio Merulo, in a prospectus of future publications to issue from his music publishing house (included in his book of intabulated ricercars of 1567, Brown, *Instrumental Music*, [1567]₂), lists a forthcoming book of ricercars by Jaches da Ferrara, a name by

TABLE 2
Disposition of Mode in Collections of Four-Voice Ricercars, 1540–1615

Collection (Author, Date; partbooks unless otherwise noted)	Modes				
	Not Labeled, Not Ordered	Labeled, Not Ordered (8- or 12-mode nomenclature)	Labeled, Ordered, Incomplete (8- or 12-mode nomenclature)	Labeled, Ordered, 1 Piece per Mode	Not Labeled, Ordered, 1 Piece per Mode (or modal category)
Musica nova (1540)	x	.	.	.	.
Buus, bk. 1 (1547)	x	.	.	.	.
Buus, bk. 2 (1549)	x	.	.	.	.
Padovano (1556)	.	8	.	.	.
Conforti (1558)	.	8	.	.	.
Bourdeney (ca. 1560)	.	12	.	.	.
Merulo (1567; tablature)	.	.	.	8	.
Merulo (1574)	x	.	.	.	.
Rodio (1575; score)	x	.	.	.	.
Valente (1576; tablature)	.	.	8	.	.
Malvezzi (1577)	.	12	.	.	.
Luzzaschi, bk. 2 (1578; ms. score)	.	.	.	12	.
Macque (?), Regensburg (?1585–1600; ms. score)	.	.	.	12	.
Macque, Florence (?1585–1600; ms. score)	.	.	.	12	.
Andrea Gabrieli (1589)	.	12 (1 out of order)	.	.	.
Stivori (1589)	x	.	.	.	.
Bertoldo (1591; tablature)	.	8	.	.	.
Andrea Gabrieli (1595; tablature)	.	.	.	12 (2 in mode 1)	.
Usper (1595)	x	.	.	.	.
Andrea Gabrieli (1596; tablature)	.	.	12	.	.
Mazzi (1596)	x	.	.	.	.
Raval (1596)	.	12	.	.	.
Stivori (1599)	x	.	.	.	.
Canale (1601)	.	.	.	12	.
Quagliati (1601)	x	.	.	.	.
Bonelli (1602)	.	.	.	8	.
Mayone, bk. 1 (1603; score)	x	.	.	.	.
Trabaci, bk. 1 (1603; score)	.	.	.	12	.
Padovano (1604; tablature)	.	.	12	.	.
Merulo, bk. 2 (1607)	x	.	.	.	.
Merulo, bk. 3 (1608)	x	.	.	.	.
Antegnati (1608; tablature)	.	.	.	12	.
Frescobaldi (1608; score)	.	.	.	12	.
Mayone, bk. 2 (1609; score)	.	12 (2 of 5 labeled)	.	.	.
Diruta, *Transilvano*, pt. 2 (1609; score)	.	.	.	12	.
Trabaci, bk. 2 (1615; score)	.	.	.	12	.
Frescobaldi (1615)	.	.	.	.	x*

*Modes 11 and 12 are substituted for 5 and 6; there are only 10 pieces.

TABLE 3
Contrapuntal Subjects in the Bourdeney Ricercars

Edition Number	Mischiati Index	Length* (in breves)	Comments	Measure	Subject(s)**
Principal Group					
1	295	201	1 subject, 2 countersubjects	1	
2	296	200	1 subject, 3 countersubjects	1	*la sol fa re mi*
3	297	132	2 subjects, the first double	1	
				76	
4	298	138	4 subjects by progressive variation	1	
				24	
				65	
				74	
5	299	131	3 subjects by progressive variation	1	
				42	
				94	

TABLE 3. *Continued*

Edition Number	Mischiati Index	Length* (in breves)	Comments	Measure	Subject(s)**
6	300	116	2 subjects, the second canzona-like; almost no learned device	1	
				91	
7	305	204	3 subjects, the last with detachable countersubjects	1	
				58	
				112	
8	306	220	4 subjects (*Ave maris stella*), the third and fourth with countersubjects	1	
				49	
				118	
				171	
9	307	200	3 subjects by progressive variation	1	
				59	
				92	

Edition Number	Mischiati Index	Length* (in breves)	Comments	Measure	Subject(s)**
10	308	252	1 double point, many learned devices	1	*(musical notation, S / A)*
11	309	240	Evolving series of 4 subjects, successive ones introduced as countersubjects to preceding ones, without sectional articulation	1	*(musical notation, T)*
				74	*(musical notation, A)*
				129	*(musical notation, A)*
				140	*(musical notation, T)*
12	310	204	1 double subject with 2 very short parts subjected to both learned device and rather free contour variation	1	*(musical notation, S)*
13	311	179	1 subject, 3 countersubjects	1	*(musical notation, A / T)*
14	312	146 semi-breves	Reworks each point of Rore's *Cantus*, with frequent admixture of the lower parts	1	*(musical notation, T2)* and so on

Appendix Pieces

Edition Number	Mischiati Index	Length* (in breves)	Comments	Measure	Subject(s)**
15	301	73	4 subjects (*Ave maris stella*)	1	*(musical notation, S)*
				24	*(musical notation, S)*
				36	*(musical notation, S)*
				51	*(musical notation, B)*

TABLE 3. *Continued*

Edition Number	Mischiati Index	Length* (in breves)	Comments	Measure	Subject(s)**
16	302	92	3 unrelated subjects	1	
				27	
				44	
17	303	71	2 subjects, the first double	1	
				37	

*Length in this edition (source is barred in longas except for M312, which is barred in breves)

**S = soprano; A = alto; T = tenor; B = bass; see introductory comments to Critical Notes for an explanation of voice names

which Brumel was known by virtue of having been court organist at Ferrara from 1532 onward. Thus we know that a collection of ricercars by Brumel existed, presumably as yet unpublished, when Brumel died in 1564.

Fourth, Brumel's son was organist in the cathedral at Ravenna in the late 1580s, the time and place where the Bourdeney codex seems to have been compiled.

Finally, Brumel's son, also named Giaches, may in fact have been the copyist-compiler of the Bourdeney Codex. Robert Judd has recently noticed what seems to be the signature of a Jacques Brunelli after one of the first pieces in the codex. The signature looks to be in the same hand that wrote "finis" after many of the other pieces in the codex, as well as most other comments and headings (see plate 2). If young Brumel were copying into his personal compendium a series of pieces that were in effect family heirlooms, we may suppose that he would not have needed to identify them.[22]

MUSICAL STYLE

I have summarized above the ways in which the principal group of Bourdeney ricercars partake in the newly defined generic style of the imitative Venetian ricercar of the 1550s, and the ways in which they alter and depart from that style. These alterations and departures—the distinctive aspects of the new Fer-

rarese style—merit more detailed attention, with reference to individual pieces in the collection.

In its thematic material the Ferrarese style tends to avoid the fourth- and fifth-oriented melodic vocabulary characteristic of the Venetians of especially the Andrea Gabrieli-Claudio Merulo generation in favor of hexachordal thought. The unusual prominence in the Ferrarese style of musical thought based on hexachord syllables is shown not only by the scarcity of triadic subjects, by the constant *inganni*, and by the occasional hexachordal inversion,[23] but also by a kind of subject that is defined exclusively by its (hexachordally conceived) pitch content—a kind of subject that is without rhythmic individuality on initial presentation (for example, a subject in even long notes) and that undergoes incessant rhythmic change.

Thus the Ferrarese style differs from the Venetian style rhythmically as well, avoiding the sharply profiled and consistently maintained rhythms of the Gabrieli-Merulo style in favor of constant permutation of a rhythmically neutral set of thematic materials. Subjects whose rhythmic character is consistent and defining are the exception in the principal group of Bourdeney ricercars; wide variation of rhythm and of metric placement of the subject(s) is a hallmark of these pieces. Though this stylistic trait is present in the earlier Venetian style of Buus and Padovano, it is carried in the Bourdeney pieces to a greater degree. Example 1 illustrates seven rhythmic transformations of the subject of ricercar 13 (M311). (Note that the transformations at mm. 21 and 51 involve *inganno* as well.) As many transformations could be shown for inverted statements of the subject.

Example 1

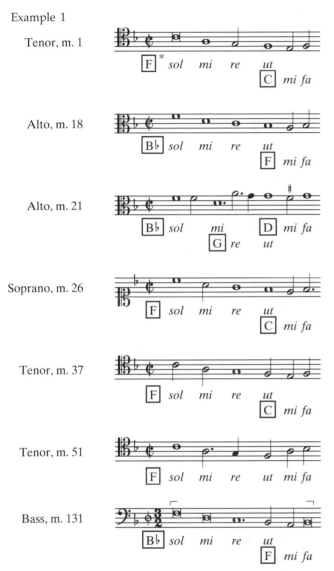

*Identifying pitch classes for *ut* in operative hexachords are boxed

In their economy of material the Bourdeney pieces exceed any collection of the century. Five of the thirteen pieces here (excluding for this purpose the ricercar based on the Rore madrigal) have one subject (nos. 1, 2, 10, 12, and 13); two have two (nos. 3 and 6); three have three (nos. 5, 7, and 9); three have four (nos. 4, 8, and 11—no. 8 treats the four phrases of *Ave maris stella* as a succession of subjects).[24]

Even when the Bourdeney pieces have a number of what my tally counts as new subjects in a succession of sections, these new subjects are almost always generated by evolving variation, most often using *in-*

ganno, inversion, or augmentation of part or all of the preceding subject or countersubject in order to produce a new shape, which is then taken as the subject of an ensuing section.[25]

A straightforward instance of such evolving variation can be seen in example 2, taken from ricercar 5 (M299).

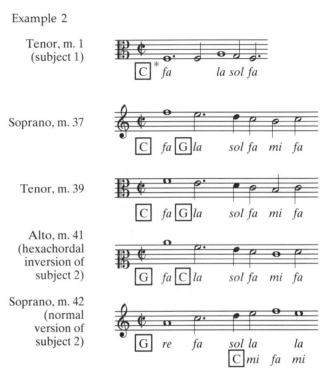

*Identifying pitch classes for *ut* in operative hexachords are boxed

If one compares the new subject, a version of which first appears in measure 37 of the soprano, with the initial subject of the piece, the process that generates the new subject is quickly revealed: first the repeated note of the initial subject is suppressed, then an *inganno* is made between the first note of the original subject, the *fa* of the natural hexachord, and the second note, which then becomes, instead of the *la* of the natural hexachord (A), the *la* of the hard hexachord (E). In a typical instance of rhythmic variation, the durational values of the subsequent *sol* and *fa* are changed; a short new tail is also added. The new version is then confirmed by the tenor, measure 39. Yet another transformation by means of an *inganno* produces a variant form in the alto, measure 41. The result is then subject to hexachordal inversion in the soprano, measure 42, to give the most characteristic guise of the subject of the ensuing section.

No matter how many subjects a piece may have, distinctive countersubjects are almost always present, either generated from the subject by motivic variation or picked out from the free voices and elevated to the status of countersubject by isolation and repetition. In the case of multisubject pieces such as numbers 8 and 11, the countersubjects often serve as binding material between sections—the countersubject of one section prefiguring the subject of the next, or the subject of one section serving also as the countersubject of the next. In pieces with only one subject (e.g., no. 13), the succession of countersubjects helps to create variety and to clarify sectional articulations.

Appendix Pieces

The particular stylistic traits described above can be found quite consistently in most of the Bourdeney ricercars. The most striking exception is the block of three pieces preceding the fully texted motet attributed to Paolo Animuccia (M301–3). A number of pieces of evidence indicates that the principal group of ricercars was interrupted for the copying of three extraneous ricercars and a motet by Animuccia, whereupon it was resumed and completed. Some of this evidence is external. For example:

—There is precedent in the codex for putting an unrelated piece or a small group of unrelated pieces in the midst of a larger, seemingly unified group. A group of motets and madrigals by Porta (M320–47) is interrupted by an unattributed motet by Merulo, an interruption that can be identified only by concordance. Similarly, a group of madrigals and motets by Rore is interrupted twice by pieces by Willaert, also without distinguishing attributions. It seems likely that the scribe entered pieces into his compendium, sometimes from circulating manuscript sources (since the order of the pieces in the codex varies from the order in surviving prints), pretty much as they became available to him.[26] We may presume that, if a particular fascicle was available to him for only a limited amount of time, he would simply enter its contents in the midst of whatever larger project was underway. If the pieces were attributed in his source, he would note the attribution; if not, he would not. The scribe seems often to put an attribution at the beginning of a group, but when he returns to an interrupted group he makes no new attribution. When there is an interruption in a group but no attribution, a change in genre often makes the interruption clear to us, as when a Striggio madrigal occurs in the midst of Palestrina's third book of masses (M264–71). Without the change in genre, often only external concordances enable one to spot an interruption.

—The first piece of the proposed interruption in the principal group of Brumel ricercars (M301) is marked not by a change in genre but by a distinctly new notational habit, presumably derived from a source different from that for the principal group, a source written by a different scribe. In this first piece of the proposed interruption, all accidentals (even including all cadential leading tones but the final one) are written out, a situation that obtains in none of the other ricercars; some ornamentation (e.g., eighth-note-turn figures) is written in as well.

—The second piece in the proposed interruption (M302) is explicitly attributed to Fabrizio Dentice, the only specific attribution in the whole group of ricercars, and one that must separate this piece from those attributed to Giaches in the Chigi fascicles.

—After a third and anonymous ricercar (M303), the proposed interruption is closed by a piece clearly extraneous to the principal group, a fully texted motet specifically attributed to Paolo Animuccia (M304).[27]

MUSICAL STYLE

The evidence of the music is equally compelling. The three pieces published here as an Appendix, numbers 15–17, are stylistically quite different from the principal group of thirteen just discussed. Most obviously, the Appendix pieces are all markedly shorter. The contrast between them and the principal group can be seen most strikingly in the two ricercars based on *Ave maris stella*: Appendix, number 15, is seventy-three breves long, as opposed to the 220 breves of number 8 in the principal group. The imitative elaborations of the four successive phrases of the hymn are twenty-one, fourteen, fifteen, and twenty-three breves long in the Appendix piece; in number 8 they cover thirty-five, eighty (including a long-note treatment of this phrase in all voices), fifty-three, and fifty breves.

From breve to breve the style of the Appendix pieces is also quite different from that of the principal group. All the Appendix pieces have a number of usually unrelated subjects. Thus their economy of material is much less. So too is their density of imitative entries. In the Appendix pieces the average length of a section on a single subject is well under twenty-five breves; a point enters only four to eight times in a section. (Even in the multisubject no. 8 from the principal group, a point enters from eleven to twenty-five times in a section.) In the long-note sections at the end of Appendix, numbers 16 and 17, imitative structure disappears almost entirely in the surrounding voices, where it is replaced by a free motivic play recalling the accompanying voices of a Ruffo capriccio or a Conforti ricercar, a style nowhere to be found in the principal group.[28] In the Appendix pieces, the subjects are long (ten to twenty notes) and have characteristic rhythmic motives and melodic contours (as opposed to the short, hexachordal subjects without characteristic rhythms of the principal group). Melodic evolving variation, where it exists at all in the Appendix pieces (the final sections of nos.

16 and 17), is rather free—that is, it does not proceed by application of the learned devices characteristic of the other pieces.

In fact, there is very little use of learned devices at all in the Appendix pieces. Number 17 is unlike the previous two in using inversion immediately in both its sections. Its sections are also longer (thirty-five and thirty-seven breves as opposed to the fourteen to twenty-eight breves of nos. 15 and 16), and it makes a slight attempt to interrelate its two sections by means of the countersubjects in the second. Thus number 17 of the Appendix pieces seems the closest in style to the ricercars of the principal group. Yet it has little of their severe intellectuality or density of thought (cf. the static, triadic noodling in mm. 14–15 and the heterophonic, parallel-motion duet of m. 40), and it has moments of clumsiness in rhythm and counterpoint (e.g., m. 64, where the first note of the subject has to be omitted for the sake of the counterpoint) that are not part of the other pieces. All these things tend to exclude it from the principal group.

There is no reason, of course, to believe that the Appendix pieces form a unified group. Each of the three may be by a different composer. The evidence of notational habits (the fully written-out accidentals) indicate that the source from which number 15 was copied had been written by a scribe different from that (or those) of the other two.[29]

Performance Practice

All of the composers of imitative ricercars between Girolamo Cavazzoni and Frescobaldi were organists,[30] and many of the early sources of ricercars are manuscript scores (such as the Bourdeney Codex) or tablatures, suitable for keyboard performance. There can be no doubt that pieces such as those in the present edition could be and often were played on the organ in the sixteenth century.

Still, early title pages make clear that they could also be played by melodic instruments and/or sung. For example, the title page of the first collection of polyphonic ricercars, *Musica nova* of 1540, reads "accomodata per cantar et sonar sopra organi; et altri strumenti" ("appropriate for singing and playing on the organ and other instruments").[31]

There was, initially at least, considerable interchange between the genres of ricercar, mass, and motet. (One might, in fact, see the early imitative ricercar as an attempt to annex for textless instrumental music the *modus dicendi* of the polyphonic high style, previously belonging to texted vocal music alone.) Evidence is plentiful to the effect that, just as ricercars were sung, so motets and mass sections were also played by instruments. To pick an example

from close to the same time as the above-cited *Musica nova* of 1540, the 1539 and 1541 editions of Gombert's first book of motets for four voices both state on their title pages, "Lyris maioribus, ac Tibiis imparibus accomodata" ("appropriate for playing on gambas and recorders of various sizes").[32] Organ performance of motets is also indicated by the presence of motets, often with only textual incipits, in score compendia such as the Bourdeney Codex, probably made by organists for their own use.[33]

In sum, there can be no doubt that ricercars were played by the organ in church, often, like motets, as musical accompaniments to sections of the mass liturgy. The place of the ricercar in the divine service has been sketched by Stephen Bonta, Anthony Cummings, and James Moore,[34] and specifications of typical liturgical roles for the ricercar are still to be seen in the titles of the ricercars in Frescobaldi's *Fiori musicali* of 1635. Nonetheless, on at least some of the occasions when ricercars were sung or played by melodic instruments such as viols or recorders, this was almost certainly in the context of secular social gatherings in academies or in the private rooms of aristocratic palaces, like those described in Doni's *Dialogo della musica* or those held in the famous Accademia Filarmonica of Verona.[35] In such surroundings, the intricate artifice of the ricercars of the Ferrarese-Neapolitan school could offer rich material for a connoisseurly discussion of instrumental music, similar to the erudite and intellectual discussions of painting and literature that took place in the Italian palaces and academies of the time. That ricercars could be analyzed in such learned, verbal terms may well have been a factor in the increasing prestige of abstract instrumental music in the later sixteenth century.

The performance of these intellectual and intricate pieces as a social activity for a small group of singers or players of melodic instruments is an activity that can be revived with pleasure today. In my personal experience, although late sixteenth-century ricercars can be and clearly were played on the organ, their intricate polyphony sounds out more clearly when emanating from four separate sound sources. This is especially true for today's hearer, who is presumably less adept at the almost exclusively linear, polyphonic listening that was habitual to the trained musician of the mid-sixteenth century.

The pitch levels at which the present ricercars are printed follow the source, which notated the pieces at the most convenient pitch level for the given mode—that is, that pitch level at which the mode can be notated with no flats or one flat in the signature. These pitch levels are not binding in any absolute sense. It is clear that absolute pitch varied widely (as much as a major third up or down) in the sixteenth century, even between places near to each other in space and time.[36] When these pieces are performed as ensemble music, modern performers adept at transposing should feel no hesitation in placing the pieces at the most comfortable level for their voices or instruments.

The tempo of such conservatively notated pieces (in ¢, with motion predominantly in quarter notes through whole notes) seems to have put the motor unit of the two-unit tactus at about the heart beat of a resting man. In a duple tactus *alla breve,* the motor unit would be the semibreve, or whole note. An average pulse beat of about sixty per minute gives a comfortable whole note = ca. 60 as a suggested tempo for numbers 1–13 and Appendix, numbers 15–17. Pieces notated in the more progressive notation of number 14 (C, with considerable essential motion in quarter notes and occasional eighth notes) had their tactus on the semibreve, or whole note, with a motor unit of a minim, or half note. Although the issue is not absolutely clear, it would seem that the motor unit of such pieces was slightly slower than that of pieces notated *alla breve;* hence half note = ca. 45.[37] Both of these tempos should be understood as median figures, however, around which tempos of a particular performance might vary according to setting, performing groups, character of the piece, and so on.

One can derive a sense of the kind of mild ornamentation—turns, trills, and passing figures idiomatic to the keyboard—that an organist of the time might have added to these pieces by looking at Claudio Merulo's ricercars published in keyboard intabulation.[38]

The Edition

In titles, ascriptions, and other aspects of the edition that use literals, square brackets enclose editorial additions, angle brackets enclose editorial expansions. In the music headings a superscript following a page number denotes the system on that page.

The incipit to each piece gives the clef, mensuration, and first note of the source. The note values of the edition are those of the source, with the following exceptions: an occasional pair of tied minims (half notes) or a semibreve (whole note) tied to a minim within the measure are replaced by a semibreve or a dotted semibreve respectively; some longer notes are divided and tied to accommodate barlines added here; and isolated triplets under duple meters are renotated in the usual way (⌐——3——⌐). In triple-meter sections the mensuration sign of the source is given above the system, and an occasional dot has been added to the breves to bring them into conformity with modern notational practice. At each inter-

nal change of mensuration, a proportional relationship is suggested.

Measures of perfect or imperfect breves are used throughout the edition, save for number 14, which is barred in semibreves to reflect the different mensuration sign in which it is notated. The source customarily uses measures of two breves, occasionally less, occasionally more. No attempt has been made here to preserve the occasional irregular measure of the original. Like measures in other late sixteenth- or early seventeenth-century scores, the barlines in the Bourdeney Codex do not have metrical meaning— that is, they do not privilege one semibreve over another. Instead, they are pragmatic means for aiding the performer or reader with matters of vertical alignment and visual orientation. All of the accidentals occurring in the source are printed within the staff in the present edition. The only changes here are that sharp signs, which are often found above or below a note in the source, have been tacitly placed to the left of the note in the edition, and that the sharp sign used to cancel a flat in the source has been tacitly replaced with a natural sign. (No natural signs occur in the source.) Accidentals in the source and in this edition are always valid only for the individual note following them. (But see the observations concerning m. 143 of no. 1 [M295] and m. 75 of no. 8 [M306] below.) A cautionary accidental is placed above the staff to cancel a preceding accidental if the note occurs again in the same measure of the edition.

Editorially recommended accidentals not specified in the source are placed above the staff. Those accidentals that would have been virtually obligatory in a stylish sixteenth-century performance are printed above the staff without parentheses. Those that are optional—either because we are not yet clear on practice at the time or because we know that they would have been optional even within a given sixteenth-century performance situation—are printed within parentheses above the staff.

Critical Notes

The four staves (for no. 14, five staves) of the systems are unlabeled in the source. For purposes of reference in these notes and throughout this Preface, the staves are referred to as "soprano," "alto," "tenor" (for no. 14, "tenor 1," "tenor 2"), and "bass," from top to bottom. "Chigi" refers to Rome, Biblioteca Apostolica Vaticana, Chigi Q.VIII.206, where ricercars 6, 5, 3, and 2 are to be found, in that order. Durations are referred to using the nomenclature of sixteenth-century notation: long, breve, semibreve (= whole note), and minim (= half note). The semiminim (= quarter note) and fusa (= eighth note) also appear in the edition but are not discussed in these notes. Pitch is indicated by the familiar system C to B, c to b, c' (= middle C) to b', c" to b".

[1] *Recercare del Nono Tuono (M295)*

M. 143, alto: the flat before note 2 (the second e') may refer to note 1 as well, or the first may be taken as flatted by the *una nota supra la* guideline—in either case, a direct chromatic reading of e'-natural e'-flat seems unlikely, since chromaticism is nowhere else part of these pieces (see also no. 8, m. 75, below).

M. 168: note that where the same change of mensuration happens in no. 8 (m. 196), a later hand has written, "Cambiamento del tempo" —see plate 1.

[2. *Ricercar sopra* la sol fa re mi] *(M296)*

Concordant source: Chigi, fols. 163r–167r ("Altra fant.a di Giaches à 4")

[3. *Ricercar del terzo tono*] *(M297)*

Concordant source: Chigi, fols. 160v–163r ("Altra fantasia di Giaches. à 4.")

M. 73, tenor: notes 2–4 are minims, the last tied to m. 74, note 1, in Chigi. M. 88, alto: note 2 is a in Chigi. M. 90, alto: note 1 is f in Chigi. M. 122, tenor: notes 2–4 are minim a, semibreve g in Chigi. M. 132, tenor: note is g-sharp in Chigi.

[4. *Ricercar del nono tono*] *(M298)*

M. 117, soprano: note 5 is b'.

[5. *Ricercar del quinto tono*] *(M299)*

Concordant source: Chigi, fols. 158r–160v ("Altra fantas.ª di Giaches")

[6. *Ricercar del dodicesimo tono*] *(M300)*

Concordance: Chigi, fols. 156r–158r ("Fantasia di Giaches a 4")

M. 96, tenor: notes 3–6 are all semiminims in Chigi.

[7] *R⟨icerca⟩re del p⟨rim⟩o T⟨o⟩no (M305)*

Mm. 9–42, tenor: as in several later instances, erasure has made the staff almost illegible, requiring much conjecture on the part of the editor. M. 12, alto: notes 2–4, erasure has made the staff difficult to read. M. 31, note 3 through m. 39, note 3, alto: erasure has made the staff difficult to read.

[8] *R⟨icerca⟩re del p⟨rim⟩o T⟨ono⟩ (M306)*

M. 75, soprano: note 2, either two flats precede this b' or the right flat was imperfectly erased and moved to the left—in either case, it seems likely that both notes 1 and 2 should be flatted since direct chromaticism seems to play no role in this style (see also the comment to [1], m. 143 above).

M. 121, tenor: rest 2 lacking; note 1 through m. 128, note 2, erasure has made the staff difficult to read (see plate 1, system 1). M. 198, soprano: no dot. M. 200, soprano: *punctum divisionis* between note 2 and m. 201, note 1. M. 214, soprano: *punctum divisionis* between note 2 and m. 215, note 1. Mm. 215–20, tenor: erasure has made the staff difficult to read.

[9] *R⟨icerca⟩re del 2do T⟨o⟩no (M307)*

M. 22, tenor: note 3 is misplaced at the beginning of the next measure. M. 29, note 1 through m. 30, note 3, soprano: erasure has made the staff difficult to read. M. 61, note 1 through m. 67, note 1, alto: erasure has made the staff virtually illegible.

[10] *R⟨icerca⟩re del 2do T⟨ono⟩ (M308)*

M. 80, tenor: note 2 is a semiminim. M. 171, alto: brevis rest lacking. M. 172, rest 1 through m. 183, note 2, alto: erasure has made the staff difficult to read.

[11] *R⟨icerca⟩re del 3o Tuono (M309)*

M. 234, tenor: note 2 is a semibreve.

[12] *R⟨icerca⟩re del 4to Tuono (M310)*

M. 89, note 1 through m. 95, note 1, alto: erasure has made the staff difficult to read.

[13] *R⟨icerca⟩re del duodecimo tuono (M311)*

Mm. 95–103, bass: erasure has made the staff difficult to read. M. 147, bass: note 2 is a semibreve—perhaps not an error but meant to be read *altera*.

[14] *R⟨icerca⟩re sopra Cantai mentre ch'i arsi ⟨di⟩ Cypriano (M312)*

M. 48, tenor 2: note 2 is c'. M. 67, note 3 through m. 77, note 4, alto: erasure has made the staff virtually illegible.

[15. *Ricercar del primo tono*] *(M301)*

M. 46, alto: notes 4–5, beaming unclear. M. 58, Soprano: note 1 is f. M. 59, note 2 through m. 60, note 2, tenor: erasure has made the staff difficult to read.

[17. *Ricercar del secondo tono*] *(M303)*

M. 68, tenor: notes 3–4 are one b-flat semibreve. M. 71, bass: note is c.

Acknowledgments

My thanks are due to the Bibliothèque nationale for permission to work in its well-equipped reading room, where I first encountered these pieces, for permitting me to consult the Bourdeney Codex there, and for supplying me with a microfilm whereby I could study its contents further; to many colleagues, most particularly James Haar and my editor, Christopher Hill, for recommending revisions in my introduction; and to the University of California for awarding me a Humanities Research Fellowship for the sabbatical semester during which I first encountered these pieces.

Notes

1. A detailed appreciation of the compositional and aesthetic subtleties of one of these pieces is found in Anthony Newcomb, "Form and Fantasy in Wert's Instrumental Polyphony," *Studi musicali* 7 (1978): 85–102. (At that point I accepted the then-current attribution to Wert.)

2. Nanie Bridgman and François Lesure, "Une anthologie 'historique' de la fin du XVIe siècle: le manuscrit Bourdeney," in *Miscelánea en homenaje a Monseñor Higinio Anglés* vol. 1 (Barcelona: Consejo superior di investigaciones científicas, 1958), 161–74.

3. Oscar Mischiati, "Un'antologia manoscritta in partitura del secolo XVI," *Rivista italiana di musicologia* 10 (1975): 265–328, is a complete inventory of the Bourdeney Codex. The present ricercars are items 295–303 and 305–12 in Mischiati's inventory.

4. On scores in the sixteenth century, see *The New Grove Dictionary of Music and Musicians,* s.v. "Score," by David Charlton, and Edward E. Lowinsky, "Early Scores in Manuscript," *Journal of the American Musicological Society* 13 (1960): 126–73.

5. Both the predominance of the works of Porta and a motet and a madrigal for local saints and civic dignitaries point to Ravenna. See Mischiati, "Un'antologia manoscritta," 266–67.

6. Bridgman and Lesure, "Une anthologie 'historique,' " 162.

7. The manuscript fascicles in question are I-Rvat MS. Chigi Q.VIII.206, fascicles 41 and 42. See Harry B. Lincoln, "I manoscritti chigiani di musica organo-cembalistica della Biblioteca Apostolica Vaticana," *L'Organo* 5 (1964–67): 78–80. On the Chigi manuscripts as a whole, see Claudio Annibaldi, "Musical Autographs of Frescobaldi and His Entourage in Roman Sources," *Journal of the American Musicological Society* 43 (1990): 393–425.

8. See Lowinsky, "Early Scores," 135–36. Plate 8 from this article reproduces the opening of ricercar 6 of this edition, as given in the Chigi fascicles.

9. Uppsala, Universitetsbiblioteket, ms Vokalmusic i handskrift 87, fol. 80v.

10. Carol MacClintock, "The 'Giaches Fantasias' in MS Chigi Q VIII 206: A Problem in Identification," *Journal of the American Musicological Society* 19 (1966): 370–82.

11. See note 1.

12. The reasoning leading to the two conclusions is laid forth in detail in Anthony Newcomb, "The Anonymous Ricercars of the Bourdeney Codex," in *Frescobaldi Studies,* ed. Alexander Silbiger (Durham, N.C.: Duke University Press, 1987), 97–123.

13. Padovano's collection (1556₉ in Howard M. Brown, *Instrumental Music Printed before 1600: A Bibliography* [Cambridge, Mass.: Harvard University Press, 1965]) is available in a complete modern edition: Annibale Padovano, *Ricercari,* ed. H. Pierront and J. P. Hennebains (Paris: Éditions

de l'Oiseau-lyre, 1934). Five ricercars from the collection are also published in Cristofano Malvezzi, Jacopo Peri, Annibale Padovano, *Ensemble Ricercars,* ed. Milton A. Swenson, Recent Researches in the Music of the Renaissance, 27 (Madison: A-R Editions, 1978). Buus's collection of *Ricercari da cantare e sonare . . . Libro primo* (1547¹ in Brown, *Instrumental Music*) is also available in modern editions: Jacobus Buus, *Orgelwerke,* vol. 2, ed. Thomas Daniel Schlee, (Vienna: Universal Editions, 1983), and Giaques Buus, *Ricercari a quattro voci: Libro primo,* ed. Donald Beecher and Bryan Gillingham, Italian Renaissance Consort Series, 5, vols. 1 and 2 (Ottawa: Dovehouse, 1983–84). Buus's *Il secondo libro di ricercare* of 1549 has been edited by James Ladewig in Italian Instrumental Music of the Sixteenth and Early Seventeenth Centuries, 3 (New York: Garland, forthcoming).

These comments on the length of ricercars from the 1540s refer to pieces printed in partbooks. The two-staff keyboard notation used for Girolamo Cavazzoni's collection of 1543 (1543₁ in Brown, *Instrumental Music*) consumes much more space and seems to dictate shorter pieces.

14. See, for example, the eight ricercars of Malvezzi in the edition cited in the previous note, all but one of which are between 84 and 104 breves in length.

15. He also misattributed the pieces to Sperindio Bertoldo—see Brown, *Instrumental Music,* 1591₄.

16. Exceptionally enough for a collection of ricercars, it had more than one edition, and pieces from it were intabulated by several lutenists, pirated in other prints even into the next century, and copied into a number of manuscript scores (including a complete manuscript copy of the print now in Brussels).

17. Numbers 2 and 8 in the present edition. The two types are combined in one piece in the Padovano collection (no. 4 in the original print and in the Pierront-Hennebains edition, no. 11 in Swenson's partial edition), which is based on the successive phrases of the Kyrie *Cunctipotens genitor deus.* Padovano in turn abstracts *la sol fa re mi* from the second phrase of the chant (mm. 21–30 in the Swenson edition). The tradition of pieces or sections of pieces built on *la sol fa re mi* goes back to the dawn of the imitative ricercar for ensemble or keyboard. Ricercar 14 by Willaert from *Musica nova* of 1540 (Brown, *Instrumental Music,* 1540₃), the first collection of ensemble ricercars, includes a long section based on *la sol fa re mi* (mm. 93–136 in the modern edition edited by H. Colin Slim, Monuments of Renaissance Music, 1 [Chicago: University of Chicago Press, 1964]). James Haar, "Some Remarks on the 'Missa La sol fa re mi,' " traces the history of this subgenre of the ricercar (in *Josquin des Prez,* ed. Edward E. Lowinsky [London, 1976], 564–88, esp. 583–88). The ricercar on *la sol fa re mi* in the present edition (no. 2) is number 2 in Professor Haar's list of instrumental pieces. He knew of the Chigi piece from the mention of the Chigi source in Lowinsky, "Early Scores"

(see n. 1 above); he also carried over Lowinsky's mistaken identification of the Chigi piece with the independent lute ricercar in the Uppsala lute tablature (see n. 9 above). Professor Haar did not note the section on *la sol fa re mi* in Willaert's *Musica nova* ricercar and in Padovano's.

18. *Inganno* is a concept, always hexachordally based, according to which the solmization syllables that would be sung to a series of notes remain the same while the melodic contour and interval content of the series is changed, sometimes drastically, by switching from one hexachord to another at various places in the series, switches not otherwise required by the rules of hexachordal mutation. The concept is exposed and developed in the context of one of the present ricercars in Newcomb, "Form and Fantasy" (see n. 1).

19. The Venetian and the Ferrarese-Neapolitan-Roman are the two principal schools of ricercar composition in the period 1550–1625. A thin but separate line of evolution is traced by the Conforti book of ricercars (1558) and Ruffo's three-voice book of *Capricci* of 1564. The pieces in this pair of publications are less sober, restrained, and learned in style than those in either the Venetian or Ferrarese schools. If one compares the four-voice pieces of Conforti with those of the Ferrarese composers, most striking is the much lesser use of learned devices in Conforti's pieces, their much lower thematic density, and their greater use of scalar, triadic, and repeated-note subjects. Belonging to no continuing school but close to the Ferrarese school in style are Cristofano Malvezzi's ricercars of 1577. Indeed, Malvezzi may have been a pupil of Giaches Brumel as a young man in the late 1550s—see the preface to Swenson, ed., *Ensemble Ricercars,* ix and xxvii n. 15.

20. See Knud Jeppesen, "Eine frühe Orgelmesse aus Castell'Arquato," *Archiv für Musikwissenschaft* 12 (1955): 193.

21. The ricercar in the Uppsala manuscript is available in modern edition in *Codex Carminum Gallicorum,* ed. Bengt Hambraeus, Studia musicologica upsaliensia, 6 (Uppsala: Almqvist & Wiksell, 1961), 133–37. One of the two ricercars by Giaches in the Castell'Arquato manuscripts is available in modern edition: Knud Jeppesen, ed., *Die italienische Orgelmusik am Anfang des Cinquecento,* 2d ed. (Copenhagen: Hansen, 1960), 2:71–72. (Jeppesen also transcribes here other ricercars by Jacopo Fogliano, Giulio Segni, and Marc' Antonio Cavazzoni as well as an organ mass by Brumel from the Castell'Arquato tablatures.) Ironically, the Brumel ricercar from the Castell'Arquato tablature (on fols. 7–9 of fasc. 1), not yet available in modern edition, is stylistically the most progressive of the ricercars in this source. In its derivation of thematic material from the opening point, in its greater reliance on a direct succession of imitative sections, in its sectional division by strong cadences, and in its occasional skillfully avoided cadence, it surpasses all the other ricercars in this extensive tablature. A complete edition of the Castell'Arquato ricercars by H. Colin Slim is projected in the series Corpus of Early Keyboard Music.

22. I wish to thank Dr. Judd for sharing this information with me in a personal communication of 31 January 1987: "On p. 12 of the manuscript I read the words at the end of the Morales motet 'finis Jacques Brunelli', looking very much like a signature." I might add that it is not uncommon in the codex to see the large gestures of the word "finis" (connected in style to the vigorous verticals closing each system) pass gradually to a more restrained style of penmanship across the first letters of the occasional comment following a piece. Nowhere else is the flamboyant style maintained right through the word following "finis" as

here, however. This, plus the illegibility of the word (Mischiati, *op. cit.,* 275, suggests "usque [?]"), may strengthen the hypothesis that the word is a signature gesture—followed after a pause by a clearer, clarifying surname.

Why sign just this piece? The scribe arrived at this characteristic way of ending a piece—vigorous squiggles at the end of each staff, followed by the word "finis"—only after the sixth piece in the codex. The "finis" became bolder and bolder after pieces 7–9 (there was no room after piece 10) and climaxed after this, the eleventh piece and the fifth of hundreds of occurrences. Perhaps he felt he had hit his stride.

23. For this term, which means inverting the subject such that the *mi-fa* half-step remains in the same place in the subject, see James Ladewig, "Luzzaschi as Frescobaldi's Teacher," *Studi musicali* 10 (1981): 241–64. For an instance, see example 2 below.

24. For this purpose, a subject is counted as an additional, new subject only if it is presented as a new thematic event in a later section of the piece, after the beginning. When a subject and a characteristic bit of accompanying material (here called a "countersubject") are presented together simultaneously in two voices at the outset of the piece, such a unit is counted as one "double point" (in agreement with Willi Apel, *The History of Keyboard Music to 1700,* trans. Hans Tischler [Bloomington: Indiana University Press, 1972], 179 and passim). When the second part of an initial subject stated in a single voice is later split off and used as a separate bit of material, the original "bipartite" subject is counted as one "double subject" (again in agreement with Apel's terminology). Both types, which occur relatively frequently in the Bourdeney pieces, are counted as one subject in the reckonings.

25. This procedure is discussed in some detail in my article cited in note 1 above.

26. Mischiati checked the musical texts of the Bourdeney Codex versions against the printed versions in only one case, the hymns of Costanzo Porta. He found the Bourdeney versions to be significantly different from the print of 1602. See Mischiati, "Un'antologia manoscritta," 274.

27. Admittedly, this motet, which fills the bottom of a page, may have been added later to use up the empty space left between the end of M303 and the beginning of M305 at the top of the next page, although the leaving of so much empty space (more than two systems) would be an anomaly in the codex.

28. Items 1564₈ (Ruffo) and 1558₁ (Conforti) in Brown, *Instrumental Music.* For modern editions, see Vincenzo Ruffo, *Capricci in musica a tre voci,* ed. Richard D. Bodig (n.p.: Ogni Sorte Editions, 1984). Giovanni Battista Conforti, *Ricercare (1558) und Madrigale (1567),* ed. Dietrich Kämper, Concentus Musicus, 4 (Cologne: Arno Volk, 1978).

29. I should also point out the small set of consistent differences between the ricercars before the proposed interruptions and those after—that the fantasies attributed to "Giaches" in the Chigi fascicles are all to be found among those before the interruption, that those after the interruption make less frequent and systematic use of inversion than those before, and that those after the interruption all carry modal labels—in order to acknowledge the possibility that the two groups may come from a different source and may represent different chronological stages in the evolution of a single style, or even of a single project.

30. What I call here the imitative ricercar is to be distinguished from the earlier, largely nonimitative ricercar in such sources as the Petrucci lute tablature prints, the Ca-

pirola lute manuscript, or the early organ tablature prints of Andrea Antico. The difference between the two types of ricercar is explained and speculations are made about its causes in Warren Kirkendale, "Ciceronians versus Aristotelians on the Ricercar as Exordium," *Journal of the American Musicological Society* 32 (1979): 1–44.

31. See 1540_3 in Brown, *Instrumental Music*. Modern edition: *Musica nova*, ed. H. Colin Slim (see n. 17 above).

32. Joseph Schmidt-Görg, *Nicolas Gombert, Kapellmeister Karls V: Leben und Werk*, 2d ed. (Tutzing: Hans Schneider, 1971), 348–49.

33. Cf. note 4 above. At the bottom of page 560 of the Bourdeney Codex, in the midst of a complete transcription (with text incipits only) of Gombert's first book of motets, for five voices, the scribe writes, "Verte ad 2da Parte [which he often does when a page turn intervenes between first and second parts] Nicolai Gombert Per li Organisti."

34. Stephen Bonta, "The Uses of the Sonata da Chiesa," *Journal of the American Musicological Society* 22 (1969): 54–84; Anthony M. Cummings, "Toward an Interpretation of the Sixteenth-Century Motet," *Journal of the American Musicological Society* 34 (1981): 43–59, esp. 50–51; James H. Moore, "The Liturgical Uses of the Organ in Seventeenth-Century Italy: New Documents, New Hypotheses," in *Frescobaldi Studies*, ed. Alexander Silbiger, 351–83.

35. See James Haar, "Notes on the 'Dialogo della Musica' of Antonfrancesco Doni," *Music and Letters* 47 (1966): 198–224. The surviving records of the Accademia Filarmonica of Verona provide ample evidence of the playing of ricercars in such academic surroundings. See Giuseppe Turrini, *L'Accademia Filarmonica di Verona dalla fondazione (maggio 1543) al 1600 e il suo patrimonio musicale antico* (Verona, 1941), 78 (purchase of the first and second books of ricercars by Buus in 1555), 134 (presence of the "fantasie recercari contrapunti à tre voci" by Willaert in an inventory of 1559, together with consorts of recorders, shawms, and cornets).

36. See, for example, Richard Sherr, "Performance Practice in the Papal Chapel in the Sixteenth Century," *Early Music* 15 (1987): 454.

37. For a discussion of these issues, see Carl Dahlhaus, "Zur Entstehung des modernen Taktsystems im 17. Jahrhundert," *Archiv für Musikwissenschaft* 18 (1961): 223–40; *The New Grove Dictionary of Music and Musicians,* s.v. "Tempo and Expression Marks," sec. 4, by David Fallows; and Dale Bonge, "Gaffurius on Pulse and Tempo: A Reinterpretation," *Musica Disciplina* 36 (1982): 167–74.

38. *Ricercari d'intavolatura d'organo . . . Libro primo*; 1567_2 in Brown, *Instrumental Music*. A brief example is given in Apel, *History of Keyboard Music*, 184. The complete collection is published in facsimile in Biblioteca musica Bononiensis, ser. 4, no. 49 (Bologna: Forni, 1982).

Plate 1. Paris, Bibliothèque nationale, Rés. Vma ms. 851, page 427 (cf. pp. 62–66 below)
Courtesy Bibliothèque nationale

Plate 2. Paris, Bibliothèque nationale, Rés. Vma ms. 851, page 12
Courtesy Bibliothèque nationale

PRINCIPAL GROUP

[1] Recercare del Nono Tuono

Mischiati 295

F-Pn Res Vma ms. 851
pp. 413¹– 414⁴

[Giaches Brumel?]

p. 414

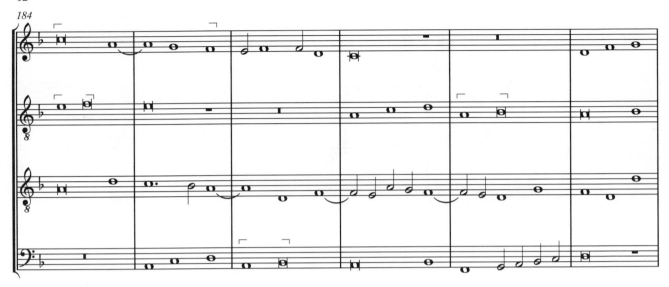

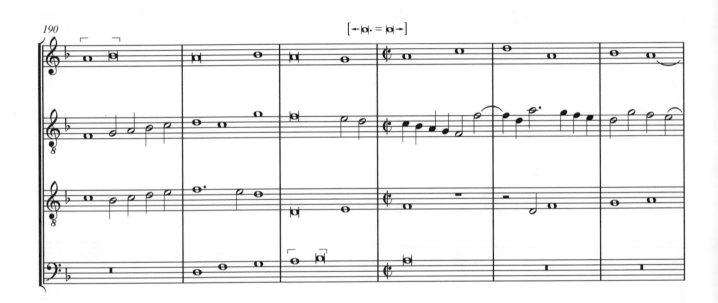

[2. Ricercar sopra *la sol fa re mi*]

Mischiati 296

F-Pn Rés Vma ms. 851
pp. 415^1– 416^3

Giaches [Brumel]

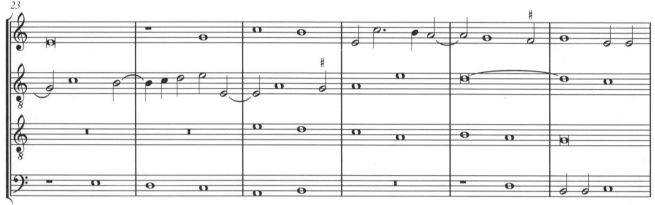

p. 416

20

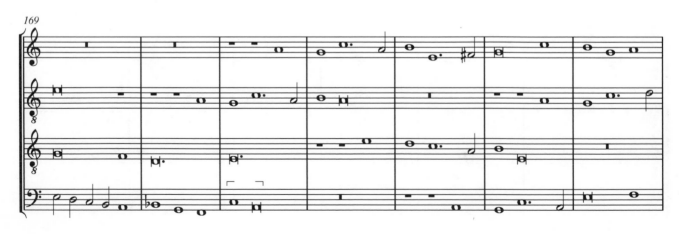

[3. Ricercar del terzo tono]

Mischiati 297

F-Pn Rés Vma ms. 851
pp. 416⁴– 417⁴

Giaches [Brumel]

p. 417

28

[4. Ricercar del nono tono]

Mischiati 298

F-Pn Rés Vma ms. 851
pp. 418^1– 419^1

[Giaches Brumel?]

p. 419

[5. Ricercar del quinto tono]

Mischiati 299

F-Pn Rés Vma ms. 851
pp. 419² – 420²

Giaches [Brumel]

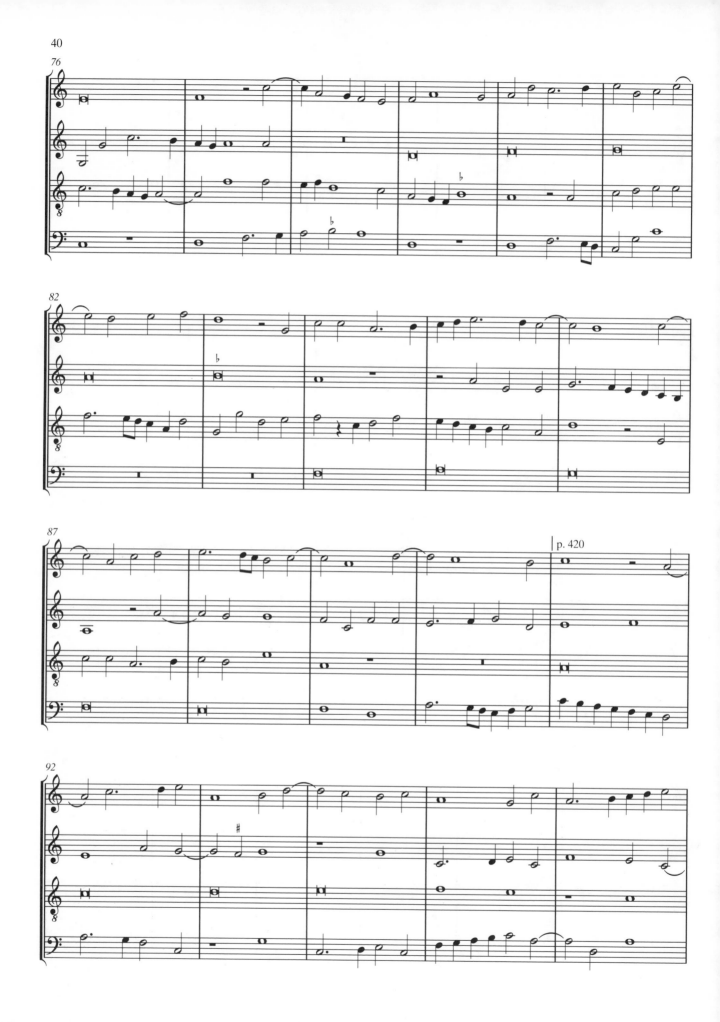

p. 420

[6. Ricercar del dodicesimo tono]

Mischiati 300

F-Pn Rés Vma ms. 851
pp. 420^2– 421^2

Giaches [Brumel]

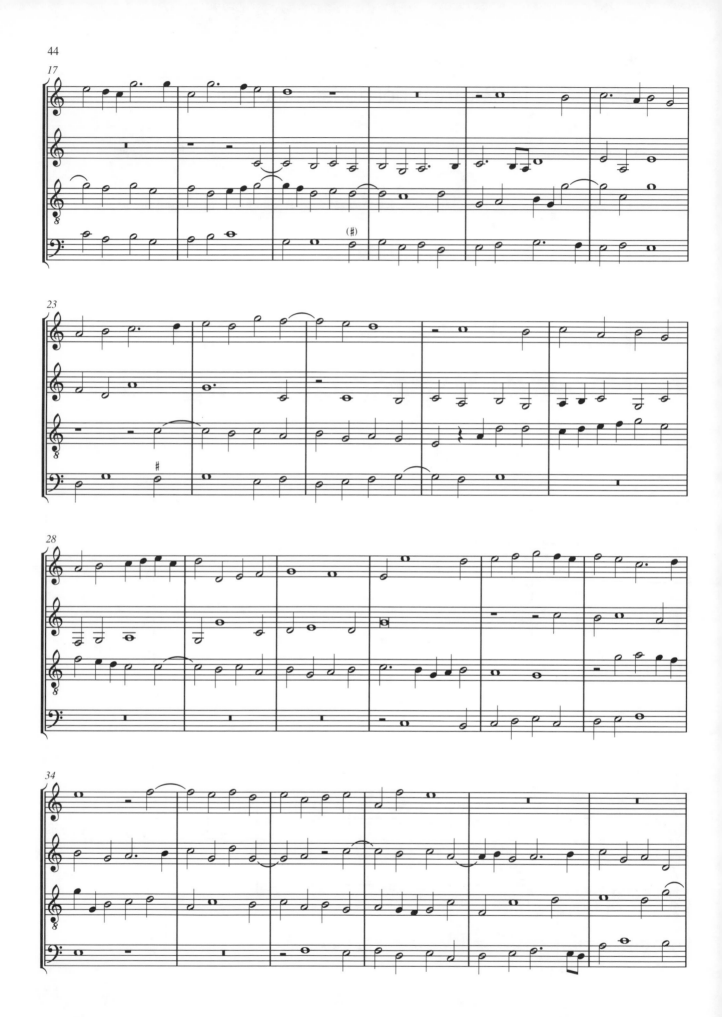

[7] R⟨icerca⟩re del p⟨rim⟩o T⟨o⟩no

Mischiati 305

F-Pn Rés Vma ms. 851
pp. 424¹– 425³

[Giaches Brumel?]

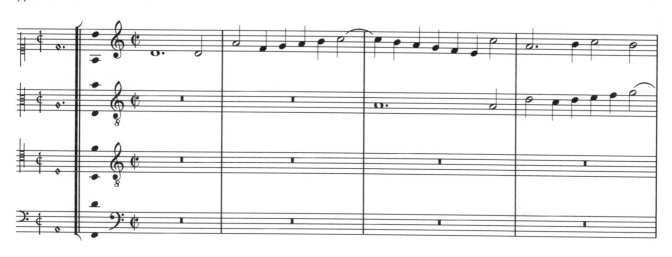

50

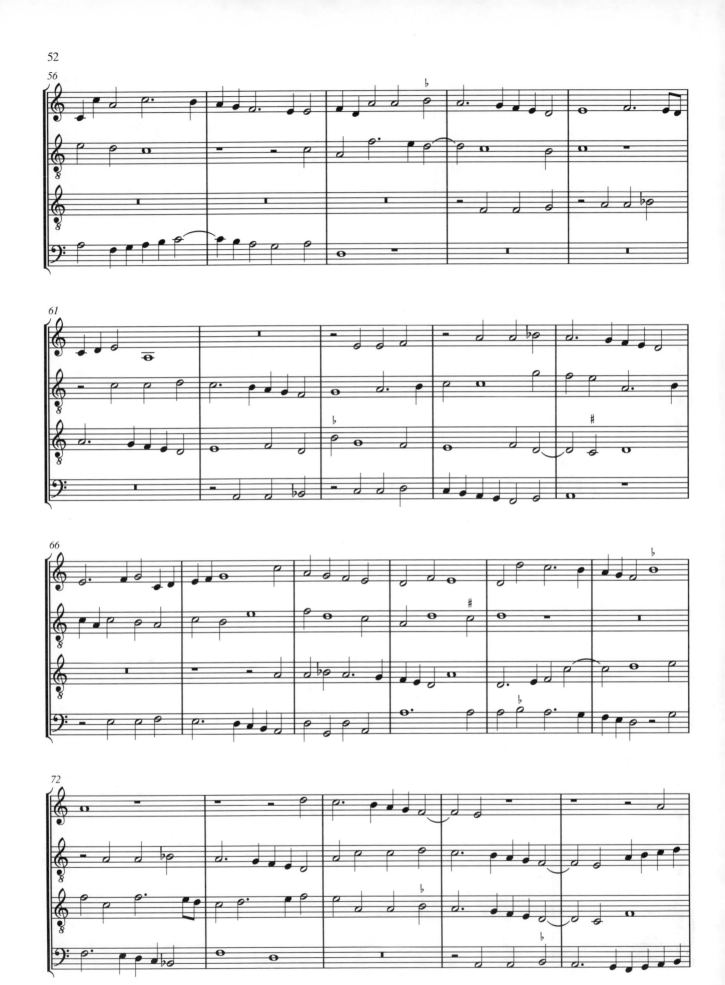

54

p. 425

56

[8] R⟨icerca⟩re del p⟨rim⟩o T⟨ono⟩

Mischiati 306

F-Pn Rés Vma ms. 851
pp. 426^1– 427^4

[Giaches Brumel?]

64

68

[9] R⟨icerca⟩re del 2ᵈᵒ T⟨o⟩no

Mischiati 307

F-Pn Rés Vma ms. 851
pp. 428¹– 429³

[Giaches Brumel?]

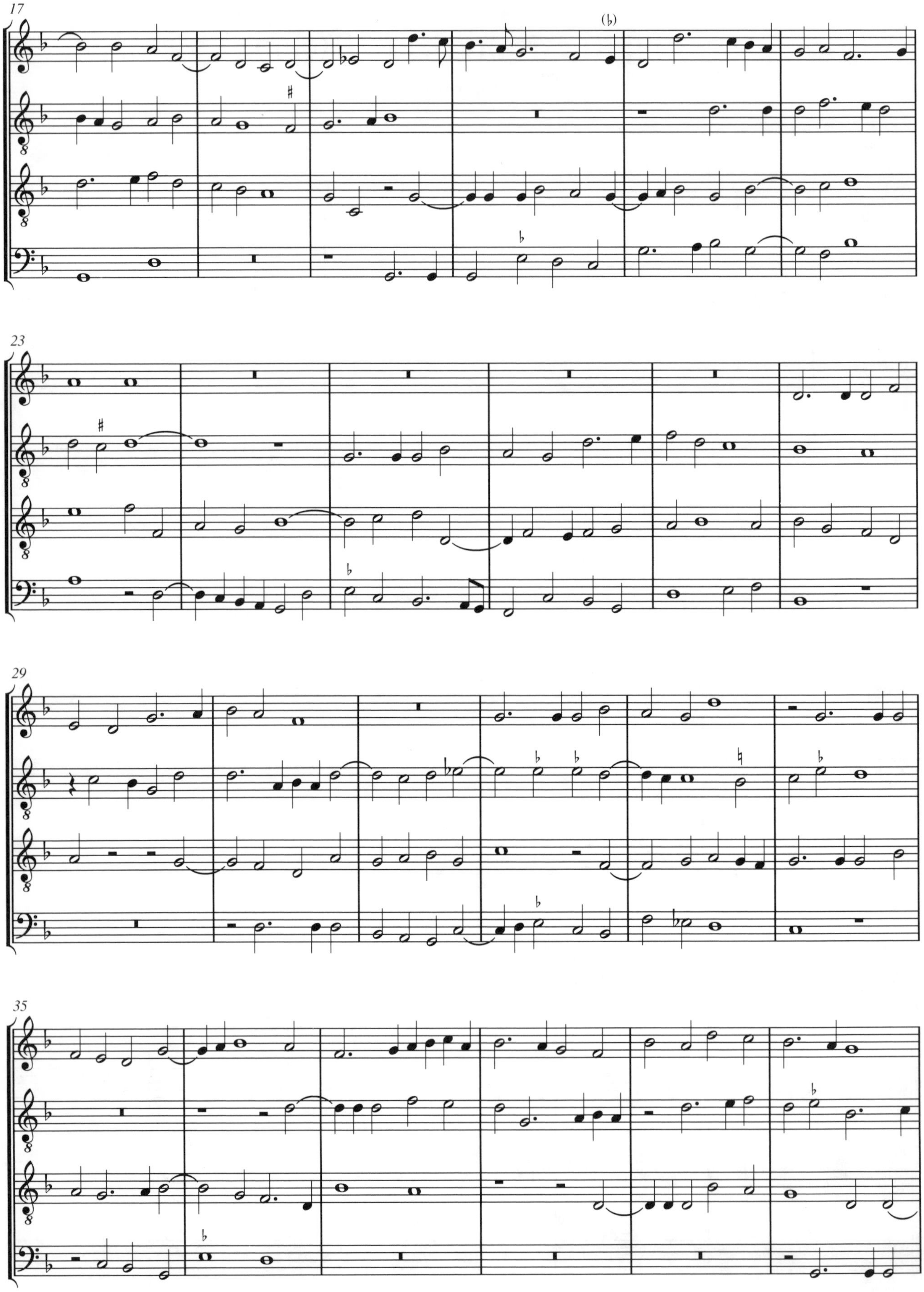
17
(♭)
23
29
35

[10] R⟨icerca⟩re del 2do T⟨ono⟩

Mischiati 308

F-Pn Res Vma ms. 851
pp. 430¹– 432¹

[Giaches Brumel?]

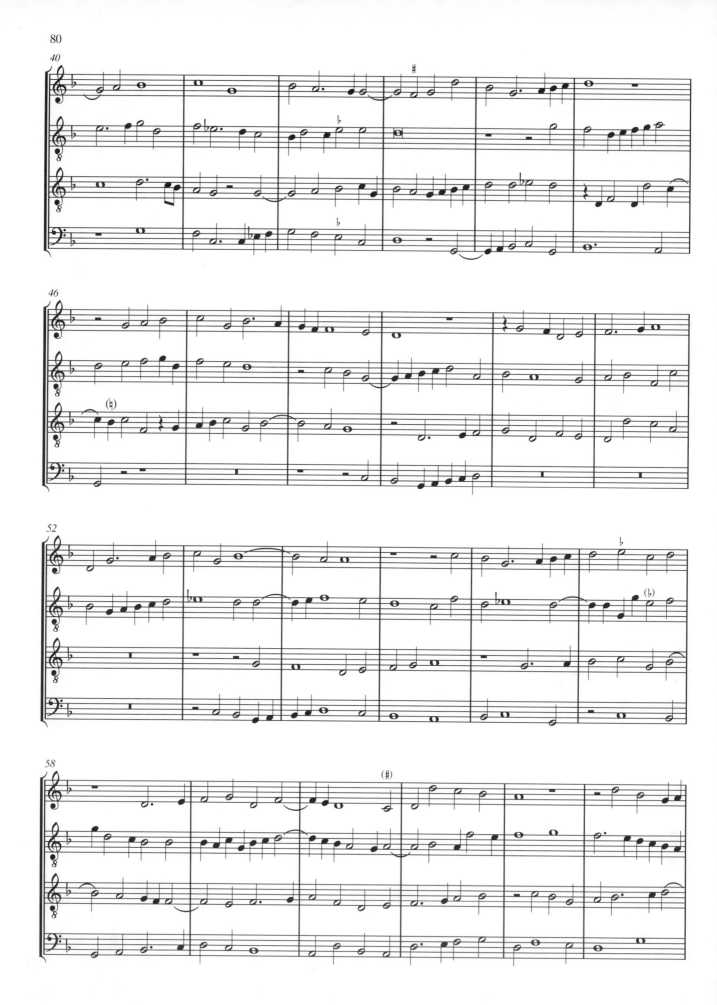

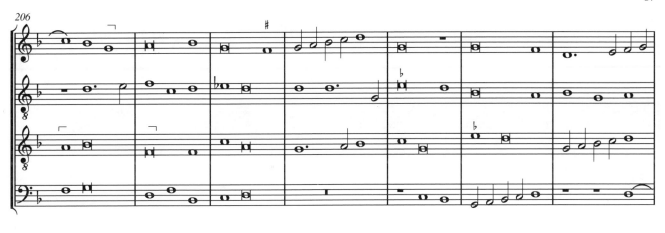

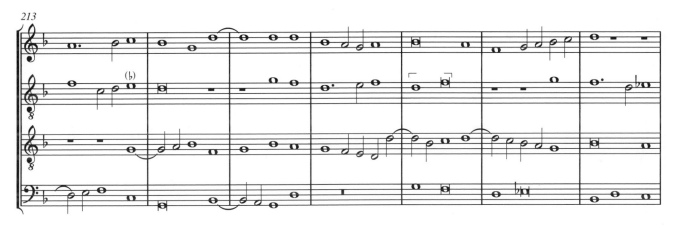

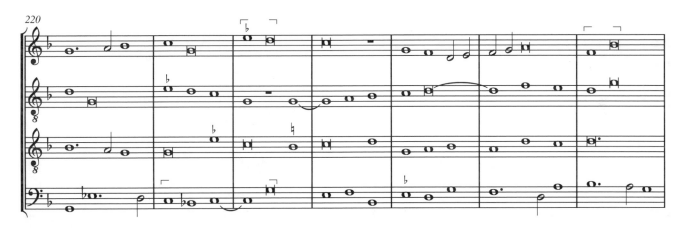

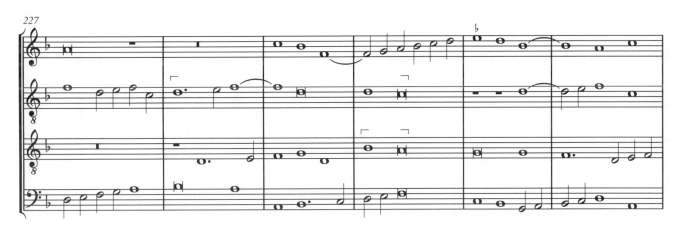

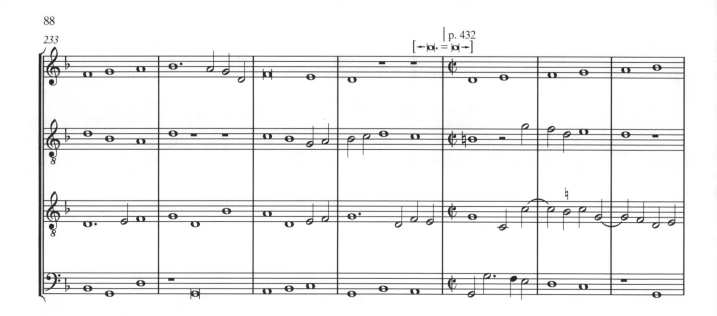

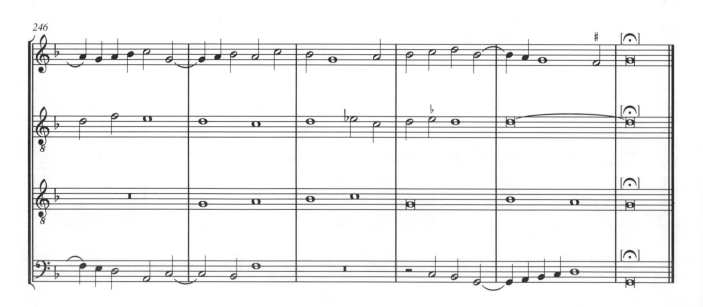

[11] R⟨icerca⟩re del 3° Tuono

Mischiati 309

F-Pn Rés Vma ms. 851
pp. 432^2– 434^1

[Giaches Brumel?]

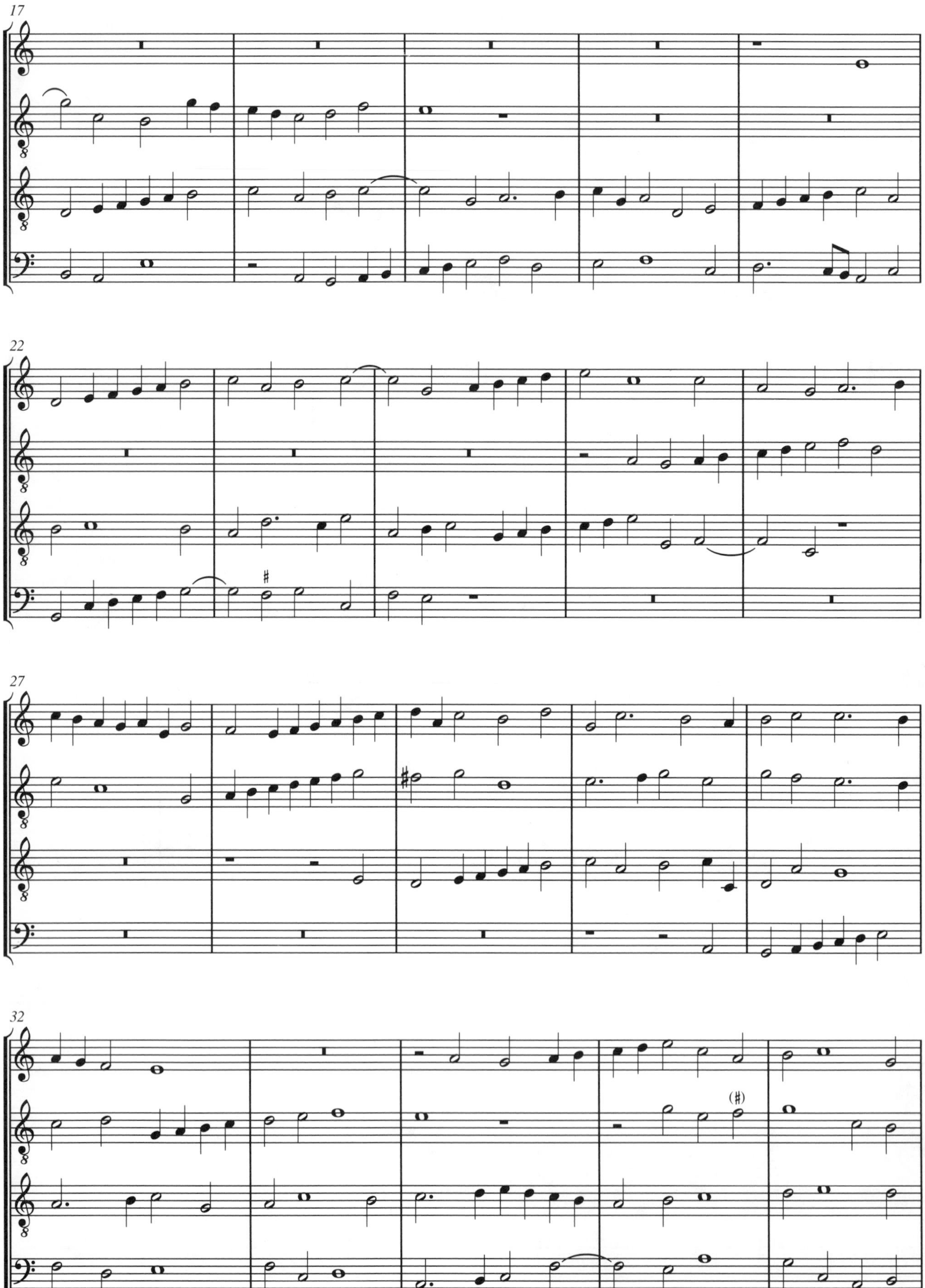
17
22
27
32

| p. 433

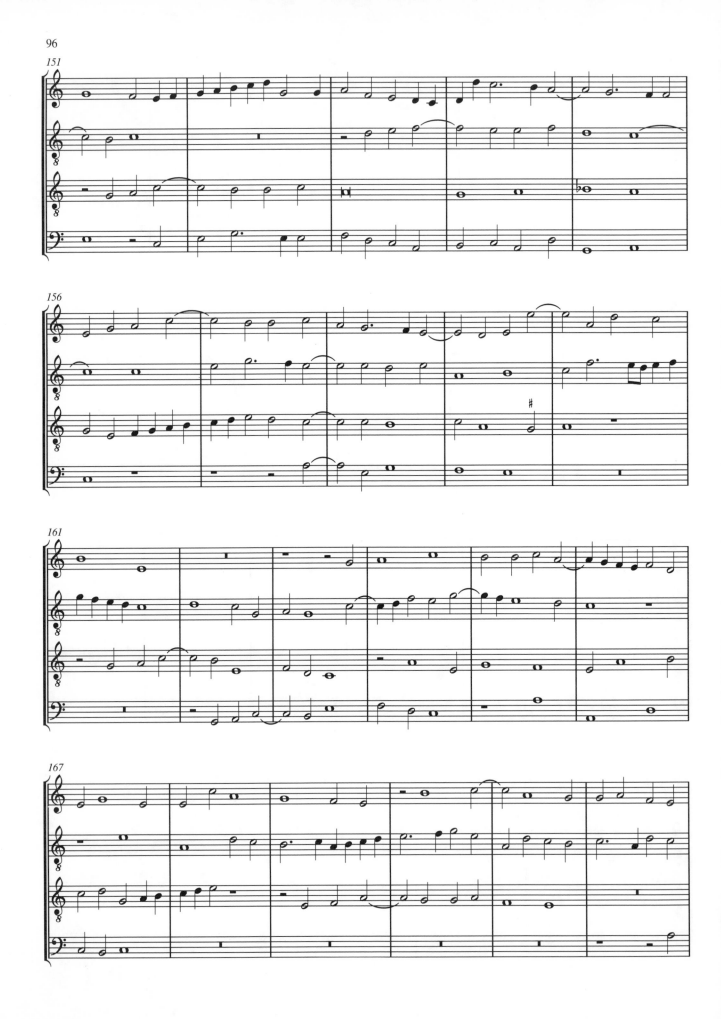

[12] R⟨icerca⟩re del 4to Tuono

Mischiati 310

F-Pn Rés Vma ms. 851
pp. 434²– 435⁴

[Giaches Brumel?]

104

p. 435

106

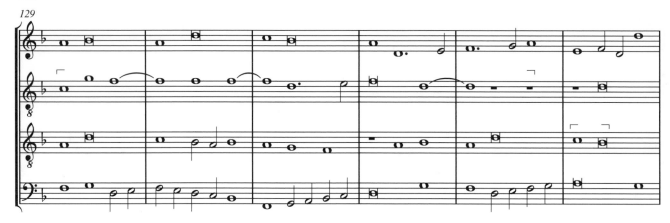

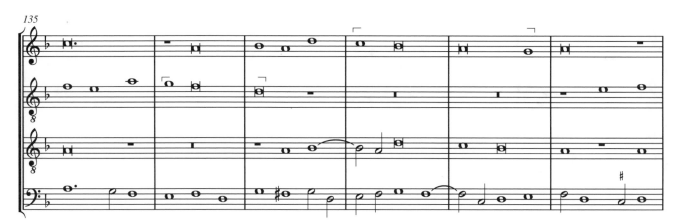

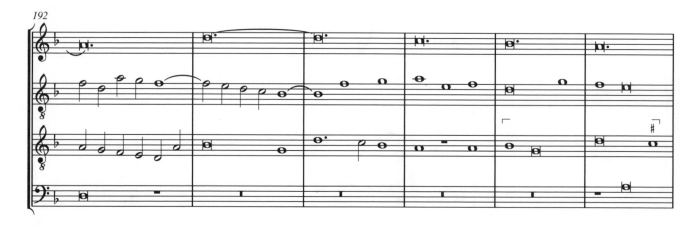

[13] R⟨icerca⟩re del duodecimo tuono

Mischiati 311

F-Pn Rés Vma ms. 851
pp. 436¹– 437²

[Giaches Brumel?]

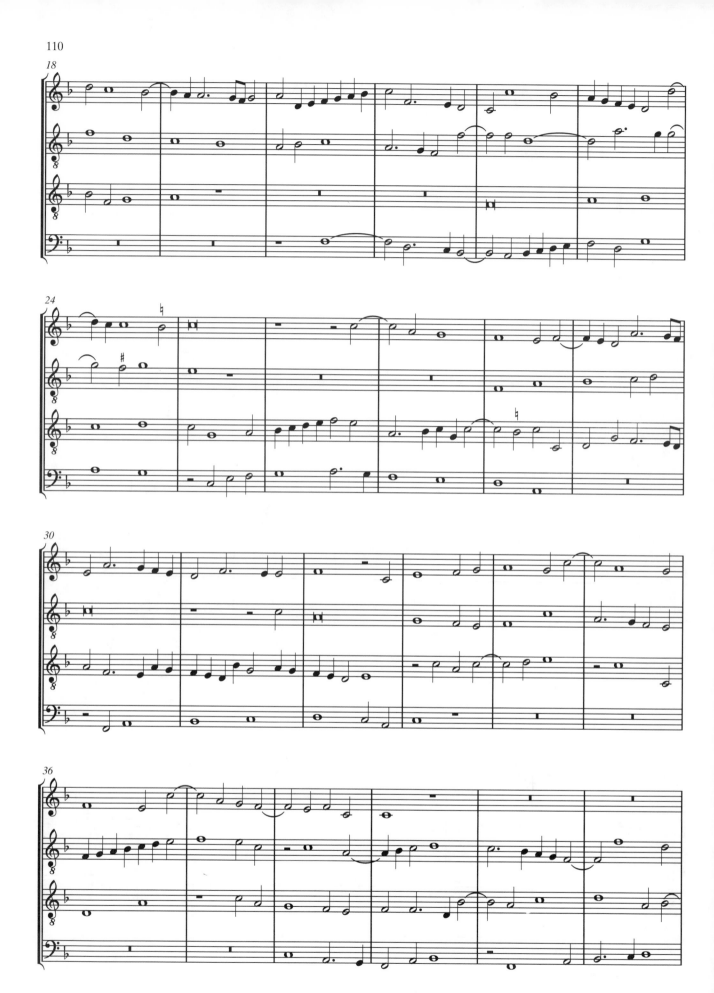

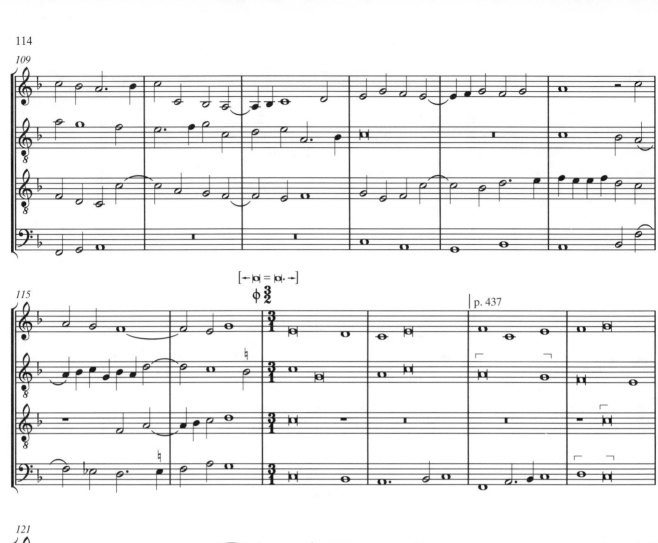

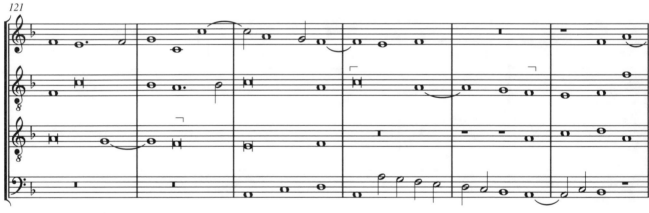

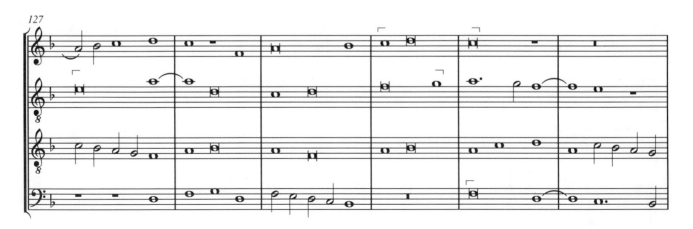

133
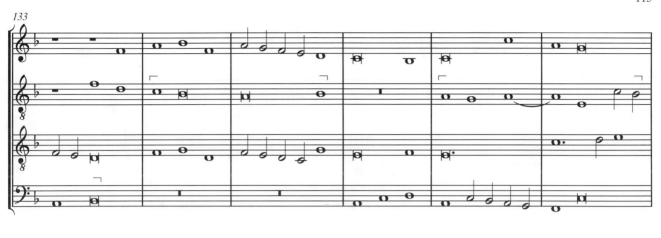

139
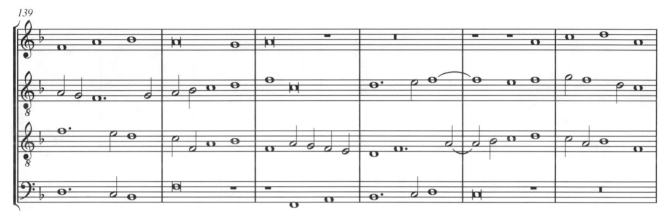

145
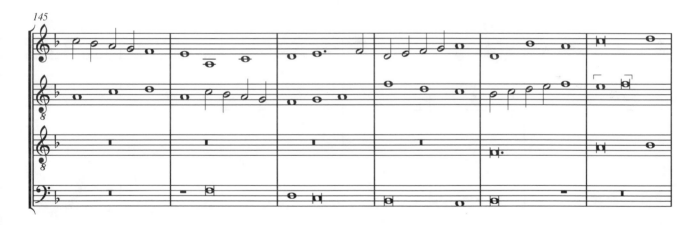

151
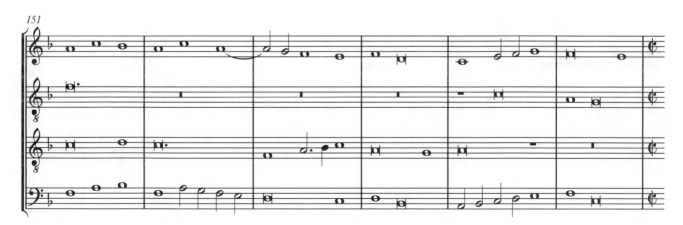

[14] R⟨icerca⟩re sopra
Cantai mentre ch'i arsi ⟨di⟩ Cypriano

Mischiati 312

F-Pn Rés Vma ms. 851
pp. 437³– 438³

[Giaches Brumel?]

p. 438

123

APPENDIX

[15. Ricercar del primo tono]

Mischiati 301

F-Pn Rés Vma ms. 851
pp. 421^2– 421^4

Anonymous

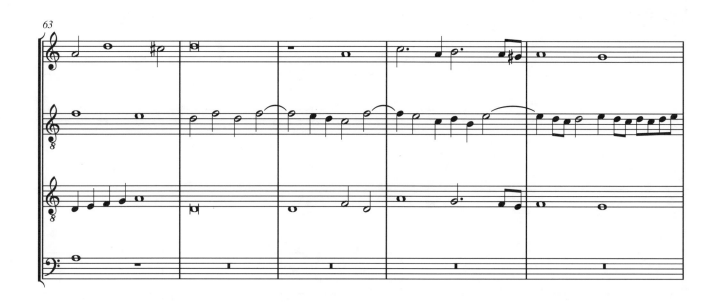

[16. Ricercar del settimo tono]

Mischiati 302

F-Pn Rés Vma ms. 851
pp. 422¹– 422³

di Fabritio Denticj

134

[17. Ricercar del secondo tono]

Mischiati 303

F-Pn Rés Vma ms. 851
pp. 422[4]– 423[2]

Anonymous